The Portal

Hussain Al Hakim

Illustrated by: Dina Al-Saffar

AuthorHouse™ UK
1663 Liberty Drive
Bloomington, IN 47403 USA
www.authorhouse.co.uk
Phone: 0800 047 8203 (Domestic TFN)
+44 1908 723714 (International)

Published by AuthorHouse 07/03/2019

ISBN: 978-1-7283-9017-8 (sc)
ISBN: 978-1-7283-9016-1 (e)

authorHOUSE®

The Portal

Hussain Al Hakim

Illustrated by: Dina Al-Saffar

One day when I was coming back home from camping, I found a giant portal. It was a huge black square, with glowing pink and purple lights in the middle. It was fascinating to see. Out of curiosity, I went into the purple and pink lights. They teleported me to the Netherworld! I couldn't see the sky, just orange and red bricks everywhere. There were also lava falls. The burning lava lit up the Netherworld. It created a thick blanket that covered the netherbrick ground. I saw zombies and zombie pigs walking in the lava. Ghosts were flying around everywhere, and train tracks ran on the netherblocks.

When the zombies saw me come through the portal, they started coming towards me to attack! I was terrified! My heart was beating so hard I thought it would come out of my chest. The zombies had ugly, green, square faces. Their eyes were all black. They had no white sclera. Scaaaaaryyyy! They wore ripped clothes, and their arms were in front of them, trying to reach for me! I screamed as loudly as I could and ran away.

I saw a mine cart on the train tracks and jumped into it.It mysteriously started to move. It went so fast I thought I was going to fly out of it. It kept going and going, until it came to a sudden stop right before the end of the tracks—and just short of a deep pit of lava.

I got out of the mine cart and saw a black netherdragon with glowing red eyes, flying towards me. The netherdragon told me it was dying because it depended on Netherworld. The Netherworld, zombies, and zombie pigs were all cursed by an evil man called Deathtrack, and he had to be stopped!

The netherdragon told me that there were four ingredients necessary to put an end to Deathtrack and his curse. I was on a mission to help the netherdragon! As soon as it told me where to find the four ingredients, I set out on my dangerous journey, not knowing what awaits me, but determined to succeed and save the Netherworld.

The four ingredients were a lava ball, a fire ball, a water ball, and a colossal sword. All the balls had dispensers which I could use to protect myself. Each could dispense a small ball of lava, fire, and water. The colossal sword was not only a sharp sword, it was also a shield.

I went into a dark cave to get the colossal sword, but it was guarded by the craken. A craken is a very large squid that eats boats … and little boys if it felt like it! I took out my small knife from my pocket to fight off the cracken, but it had eight tentacles! I tried to fight all eight tentacles, but one of them had the colossal sword. I managed to cut off seven tentacles, but the eighth fought with the colossal sword. I fought with all my strength and was finally able to cut off the last tentacle, and the craken died. I collected the colossal sword and was on my way to get the next ingredient.

I made my way to get the fire ball, but it was guarded by a sperm whale. I got out the colossal sword and tried to cut off the whale's fins. But instead, I cut off its tail. It couldn't move! I cut off its right and left fins, and it died. I collected the fire ball and moved on to get the third ingredient.

I went to find the third ingredient, the lava ball, but it was guarded by a tiger. The tiger saw me and threw lava at me. It came close but didn't touch me. The lava was worse than the fire ball because when it landed, it made a giant lava puddle. I used the colossal sword to shield myself from the lava. That way, I was able to get closer to the tiger and cut its head off. I took the lava ball and went to get the final ingredient.

The last ingredient was water, and it was protected by a very fierce lion. The lion threw water at me to distract me so it could kill me. I got out the lava ball and dispensed small lava balls to protect myself. Even though I had the lava balls, I still needed to dodge the water the lion threw at me. I got a clear shot of the lion and threw a small lava ball at it. It went right in the middle of the lion's body and died. I took the water ball and ran back to the netherdragon with all four ingredients.

The netherdragon told me that it needed to connect all four ingredients together, starting from the colossal sword. It told me that in order to break Deathtrack's curse and restore order in Netherworld, I had to stab the colossal sword in the middle ground. Knowing my final mission, I got on the netherdragon's back and we flew to the middle ground of Netherworld. I did as the netherdragon told me...and as soon as I put the sword into the ground, the skies started to clear and the lava dried and became ash. Ordinary life was restored in Netherworld!!!I got on the netherdragon's back, and it flew me to the portal to return to my home sweet home! What an adventure!

Printed in the United States
By Bookmasters